THE TALE OF
MRS. TITTLEMOUSE

BY BEATRIX POTTER

FREDERICK WARNE

ONCE upon a time there was a wood-mouse, and her name was Mrs. Tittlemouse.

She lived in a bank under a hedge.

NELLIE'S LITTLE BOOK

FREDERICK WARNE

Published by the Penguin Group
Registered office: 80 Strand, London, WC2R 0RL
Penguin Young Readers Group, 345 Hudson Street, New York, N.Y. 10014, USA

First published 1910 by Frederick Warne
This edition with new reproductions of Beatrix Potter's book illustrations first published 2007
This edition copyright © Frederick Warne & Co. 2007
Reissued 2016
New reproductions of Beatrix Potter's book illustrations copyright © Frederick Warne & Co. 2002
Original copyright in text and illustrations © Frederick Warne & Co., 1910

Frederick Warne & Co. is the owner of all rights, copyrights and trademarks
in the Beatrix Potter character names and illustrations.

Manufactured in China

Special Markets ISBN 978-0-723-26005-9

SUCH a funny house! There were yards and
yards of sandy passages, leading to storerooms
and nut-cellars and seed-cellars, all amongst the
roots of the hedge.

THERE was a kitchen, a parlour, a pantry, and a larder.

Also, there was Mrs. Tittlemouse's bedroom, where she slept in a little box bed!

MRS. TITTLEMOUSE was a most terribly
tidy particular little mouse, always sweeping
and dusting the soft sandy floors.

Sometimes a beetle lost its way in the passages.

"Shuh! shuh! little dirty feet!" said Mrs.
Tittlemouse, clattering her dust-pan.

AND one day a little old woman ran up and down in a red spotty cloak.

"Your house is on fire, Mother Ladybird! Fly away home to your children!"

ANOTHER day, a big fat spider came in
to shelter from the rain.

"Beg pardon, is this not Miss Muffet's?"

"Go away, you bold bad spider! Leaving ends
of cobweb all over my nice clean house!"

She bundled
the spider out
at a window.

He let himself
down the hedge
with a long thin
bit of string.

MRS. TITTLEMOUSE went on her way to
a distant storeroom, to fetch cherry-stones and
thistle-down seed for dinner.

All along the passage she
sniffed, and looked at the
floor.

"I smell a smell of honey; is it
the cowslips outside, in the hedge?
I am sure I can see the marks of little
dirty feet."

Suddenly round a corner, she met Babbitty
Bumble — "Zizz, Bizz, Bizzz!" said the bumble bee.

Mrs. Tittlemouse looked at her severely. She
wished that she had a broom.

"Good-day, Babbitty Bumble; I should be glad to
buy some beeswax. But what are you doing down
here? Why do you always come in at a window, and
say Zizz, Bizz, Bizzz?" Mrs. Tittlemouse began to
get cross.

"ZIZZ, Wizz, Wizz!" replied Babbitty Bumble in a peevish squeak. She sidled down a passage, and disappeared into a storeroom which had been used for acorns.

Mrs. Tittlemouse had eaten the acorns before Christmas; the storeroom ought to have been empty.

But it was full of untidy dry moss.

MRS. TITTLEMOUSE began to pull out the moss. Three or four other bees put their heads out, and buzzed fiercely.

"I am not in the habit of letting lodgings; this is an intrusion!" said Mrs. Tittlemouse. "I will have them turned out — " "Buzz! Buzz! Buzzz!" — "I wonder who would help me?" "Bizz, Wizz, Wizzz!"

— "I will not have Mr. Jackson; he never wipes his feet."

MRS. TITTLEMOUSE decided to leave the bees till after dinner.

When she got back to the parlour, she heard some one coughing in a fat voice; and there sat Mr. Jackson himself!

He was sitting all over a small rocking-chair, twiddling his thumbs and smiling, with his feet on the fender.

He lived in a drain below the hedge, in a very dirty wet ditch.

"HOW do you do, Mr. Jackson? Deary me, you have got very wet!"

"Thank you, thank you, thank you, Mrs. Tittlemouse! I'll sit awhile and dry myself," said Mr. Jackson.

He sat and smiled, and the water dripped off his coat tails. Mrs. Tittlemouse went round with a mop.

HE sat such a while that he had to be asked if he would take some dinner?

First she offered him cherry-stones. "Thank you, thank you, Mrs. Tittlemouse! No teeth, no teeth, no teeth!" said Mr. Jackson.

He opened his mouth most unnecessarily wide; he certainly had not a tooth in his head.

THEN she offered him thistle-down seed —
"Tiddly, widdly, widdly! Pouff, pouff, puff!"
said Mr. Jackson. He blew the thistle-down all
over the room.

"Thank you, thank you, thank you, Mrs.
Tittlemouse! Now what I really — *really* should
like — would be a little dish of honey!"

"I AM afraid I have not got any, Mr. Jackson!" said Mrs. Tittlemouse.

"Tiddly, widdly, widdly, Mrs. Tittlemouse!" said the smiling Mr. Jackson. "I can *smell* it; that is why I came to call."

Mr. Jackson rose ponderously from the table, and began to look into the cupboards.

Mrs. Tittlemouse followed him with a dish-cloth, to wipe his large wet footmarks off the parlour floor.

WHEN he had convinced himself that there was
no honey in the cupboards, he began to walk down
the passage.

"Indeed, indeed, you will stick fast, Mr. Jackson!"

"Tiddly, widdly, widdly, Mrs. Tittlemouse!"

FIRST he squeezed into the pantry.

"Tiddly, widdly, widdly? no honey? no honey, Mrs. Tittlemouse?"

There were three creepy-crawly people hiding in the plate-rack. Two of them got away; but the littlest one he caught.

Then he squeezed into the larder. Miss Butterfly was tasting the sugar; but she flew away out of the window.

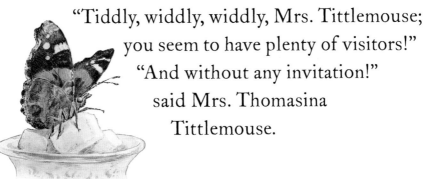

"Tiddly, widdly, widdly, Mrs. Tittlemouse; you seem to have plenty of visitors!"

"And without any invitation!" said Mrs. Thomasina Tittlemouse.

THEY went along the sandy passage —
"Tiddly widdly — " "Buzz! Wizz! Wizz!"

He met Babbitty round a corner, and snapped
her up, and put her down again.

"I do not like bumble bees. They are all over
bristles," said Mr. Jackson, wiping his mouth
with his coat-sleeve.

"Get out, you nasty old toad!" shrieked
Babbitty Bumble.

"I shall go distracted!" scolded Mrs. Tittlemouse.

SHE shut herself up in the nut-cellar while Mr. Jackson pulled out the bees-nest. He seemed to have no objection to stings.

When Mrs. Tittlemouse ventured to come out — everybody had gone away.

But the untidiness was something dreadful — "Never did I see such a mess — smears of honey; and moss, and thistle-down — and marks of big and little dirty feet — all over my nice clean house!"

SHE gathered up the moss and the remains of the beeswax.

Then she went out and fetched some twigs, to partly close up the front door.

"I will make it too small for Mr. Jackson!"

SHE fetched soft soap, and flannel, and a new scrubbing brush from the storeroom. But she was too tired to do any more. First she fell asleep in her chair, and then she went to bed.

"Will it ever be tidy again?" said poor Mrs. Tittlemouse.

NEXT morning she got up very early and began a spring cleaning which lasted a fortnight.

She swept, and scrubbed, and dusted; and she rubbed up the furniture with beeswax, and polished her little tin spoons.

WHEN it was all beautifully neat and clean, she gave a party to five other little mice, without Mr. Jackson. He smelt the party and came up the bank, but he could not squeeze in at the door.

SO they handed him out acorn-cupfuls of honeydew through the window, and he was not at all offended.

He sat outside in the sun, and said — "Tiddly, widdly, widdly! Your very good health, Mrs. Tittlemouse!"